THE 169-STOREY TREEHOUSE

Andy Griffiths lives in a 169-storey treehouse with his friend Terry and together they make funny books, just like the one you're holding in your hands right now. Andy writes the words and Terry draws the pictures. If you'd like to know more, read this book (or visit www.andygriffiths.com.au).

Terry Denton lives in a 169-storey treehouse with his friend Andy and together they make funny books, just like the one you're holding in your hands right now. Terry draws the pictures and Andy writes the words. If you'd like to know more, read this book (or visit www.terrydenton.com.au).

THE 169-STOREY TREEHOUSE

BY

ANDY GRIFFITHS

& TERRY DENTON

MACMILLAN CHILDREN'S BOOKS

First published 2023 by Pan Macmillan Australia Pty Limited

First published in the UK 2023 by Macmillan Children's Books
an imprint of Pan Macmillan
The Smithson, 6 Briset Street, London EC1M 5NR
EU representative: Macmillan Publishers Ireland Ltd, 1st Floor,
The Liffey Trust Centre, 117–126 Sheriff Street Upper
Dublin 1, D01 YC43
Associated companies throughout the world
www.panmacmillan.com

ISBN 978-1-5290-9714-6

1 3 5 7 9 8 6 4 2

A CIP catalogue record for this book is available from the British Library.

Printed and bound by CPI Group (UK) Ltd, Croydon CR0 4YY

CONTENTS

CHAPTER 1

THE 169-STOREY TREEHOUSE

Hi, my name is Andy.

This is my friend Terry.

We live in a tree.

Well, when I say 'tree', I mean treehouse. And when I say 'treehouse', I don't just mean any old treehouse—I mean a *169-storey* treehouse. (It used to be a 156-storey treehouse, but we've added another 13 storeys.)

So what are you waiting for?
Come on up!

5

GRO

ALINE

We've added a Santa Land (where it's always Christmas, thanks to all the Santa clones left over from the last book),

a potato-powered translation transmitter (it can translate any language into any other language—for animals, vegetables or minerals),

an electric pony stable with a fast-charging station and automatic hoof polishers,

a MONSTER LEVEL
(but I'm not sure this was such a good idea),

a hall of funhouse mirrors,

15

a kangaroo-riding range,

a WHATEVER-WEATHER-YOU-WANT
dome (you can have whatever weather you want
whenever you want it),

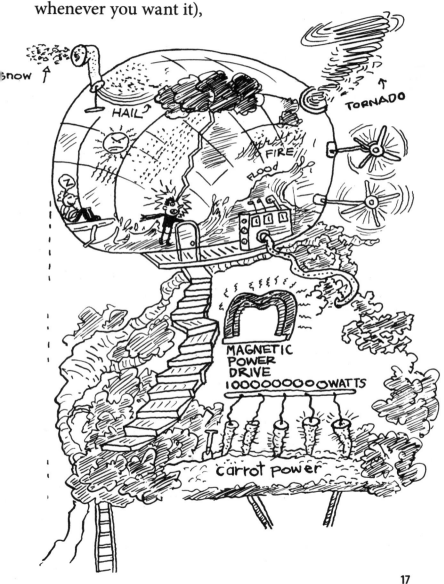

a gingerbread house (where a nice little old
lady lives),

a paper plane research and development facility
(or PPRDF for short),

QUACK

FLING SPRING

21

a treehouse (yeah, that's right, we've got a
treehouse *in* our treehouse!),

and the 169th storey (we haven't actually decided
what we're going to put on here yet, but we'll think
of something).

As well as being our home, the treehouse is where we make books together. I write the words and Terry draws the pictures.

As you can see, we've been doing this for quite a while now.

Things don't always go to plan, of course …
especially when we have to deal with things like

man-eating
mermaids,

headless
pirates,

ruthless
un-inventors,

angry vegetables,

malfunctioning
time machines,

mooovie-idea-stealing
spy cows,

whirling whirlpools,

giant feet,

angry story police,

 giant flying eyeballs,

hideous
hobyahs,

 and evil snowmen.

Oh, and I haven't
even mentioned
the giant gorilla,

the angry
Bignoseasaurus

or Terry's three-month-
long baths!

But no matter what happens, we always get our
book done in the end!

CHAPTER 2

WILD WEATHER

If you're like most of our readers, you're probably wondering why I'm still in bed. Well, it's Monday morning, and I love a good Monday morning sleep-in.

Uh-oh. Looks like rain. But that's not a problem. Fortunately, I have my emergency Monday morning sleep-in umbrella right here.

Ah, that's better. Nice and warm and dry.

Actually, now it's a little *too* warm because the rain has stopped and the sun's come out. And when I say 'the sun's come out', I mean the sun has really come out—it's actually really, really hot!

Eeek! My umbrella just caught fire. See?
I told you it was hot!

Now it's started raining again! Which is kind of
good because it's put out the fire ... but it's also
kind of bad because now it's raining so hard
I really *need* an umbrella ...

Oh, great—the wind just blew all the blankets off my bed. This is the most unrelaxing Monday morning sleep-in ever!

And then it gets even more unrelaxing when, with a loud WHUMP and a high-pitched EEK, Jill lands on my bed!

'Jill?' I say. 'What are you doing here?'

'I don't know!' she says. 'One moment I was having a lovely indoor picnic with my animals, then the next thing I knew, there was this huge storm and it blew my cottage away. And then it blew me away as well and I landed here!'

Suddenly, Terry crashes down onto the bed beside us.

'Terry?!' I say. 'Did the storm blow you here as well?'

'Sort of,' says Terry. 'You see, I thought it would be nice to start the day with a little rain shower. So I went to the WHATEVER-WEATHER-YOU-WANT dome and turned on the rain, and then I wanted to get dry so I turned on a good, strong, hot wind, but I got *too* hot, so I turned on the snow to cool off, but then there was too much snow and it turned into a blizzard, so I turned on a tornado to blow it away, but it blew *me* away instead and here I am.'

'Did you remember to shut the door before you started the weather?' I say.

'No,' says Terry. 'Was I supposed to?'

'OF COURSE YOU WERE!' I say.

'How was I supposed to know that?' says Terry.

'Because I put up a sign!' I say.

'I forgot to read it,' says Terry. 'You should have put up a sign to remind me.'

'I DID,' I say.

DON'T FORGET TO READ
THE FIRST SIGN TELLING YOU
NOT TO FORGET TO SHUT THE DOOR
BEFORE YOU START THE WEATHER UP!

(This
DEFINITELY
means you,
Terry!)

BY ORDER OF ANDY

'I forgot to read that one as well,' says Terry. 'You should have put up another sign telling me not to forget to read the second sign.'

'*I DID!!!*' I yell.

DON'T FORGET TO READ THE SECOND SIGN TELLING YOU NOT TO FORGET TO READ THE FIRST SIGN TELLING YOU NOT TO FORGET TO SHUT THE DOOR BEFORE YOU START THE WEATHER UP!
(This definitely absolutely positively means **YOU**, Terry!)

BY ORDER OF ANDY

'I forgot to read that one as well,' says Terry. 'You should have—'

RING RING
RING RING
RING RING

'That will be Mr Big Nose,' I say. 'But don't answer it—we don't have time to talk to him right now.'

'Oh yes you do!' says Mr Big Nose, answering his own call.

'What are you chuckleheads up to?' he shouts.
'The city—including my office—is being battered
by every type of weather there is and it all appears
to be coming directly from your treehouse.'

'It's Terry's fault,' I say. 'He left the door to the WHATEVER-WEATHER-YOU-WANT dome open and all the weather got out.'

'I don't care *whose* fault it is,' says Mr Big Nose. 'You've created a once-in-a-millennium meteorological disaster! Just fix it—and fast!'

'Sure thing, Mr Big Nose,' I say. 'Terry will go and shut the door right now.'

'Why do I have to do it?' says Terry.

'Because you're the one who left it open,' I say.

'I had a feeling you were going to say that,' says Terry.

'Then why did you ask?' I say.

'Because I was hoping you wouldn't,' he says.

Terry gets up onto the branch …

and starts slowly—and bravely—climbing towards
the dome.

But the higher he climbs, the slower he goes, because of all the weather blasting out of the weather dome door.

'I can't go any further!' says Terry. 'There's too much weather!'

'I think he needs a push,' says Jill. 'Come on, Andy!'

'But that's not fair!' I say. 'He's the one who left the door open!'

'I know,' says Jill. 'But he can't do it alone.'

So we climb up and start pushing.

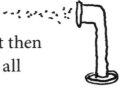

We push him a little further along, but then an extra-strong blast of wind sends us all tumbling back down the branch.

'It's impossible,' says Terry.

'Nothing's impossible,' says Jill.

'What about impossible things?' says Terry. 'They're impossible.'

'True,' says Jill. 'But this is not one of them. We just need more pushers. Let's ask everyone in the treehouse and the forest to come and help.'

'But that will take too long,' I say. 'And the longer we wait, the more weather will get out.'

'You're right,' says Jill. She frowns. 'If only we had some sort of device that could broadcast an urgent message to everybody in every possible language at a volume loud enough for them all to hear at the same time.'

'We do!' says Terry. 'That's exactly what our new potato-powered translation transmitter does!'

'That sounds perfect!' says Jill. 'To the potato-powered translation transmitter level. There's not a moment to lose!'

CHAPTER 3

THE BIG PUSH

Luckily, the potato-powered translation transmitter level is right above us, so it's not *too* hard to get there.

We set the controls to ALL LANGUAGES, ALL CREATURES, VERY LOUD and Jill begins speaking …

Jill has only just finished speaking when Terry points excitedly at the animals streaming towards us from the forest.

'It's working!' says Terry. 'Look— here they come!'

The residents of the treehouse join us too, and soon our tree is filled with an army of willing pushers.

We all line up behind Terry and push …

'Go, Terry!' I shout.

We push and push and push …

Terry gets closer and closer.

'I'm almost there!' Terry shouts back. 'But I still can't quite …'

'You've got this, Terry!' says Jill. 'You just need one last big push! Everybody ready?'

ONE… BIG… PUSH!

With the power of the last big push, Terry manages to get close enough to the weather dome door to slam it firmly shut!

'We did it!' I say. 'All the weather is back in the weather dome where it belongs.'

A big cheer rises up from below, where a large crowd has gathered.

'Hey, look!' says Terry, waving. 'There are television cameras down there. We're famous!'

'How does it feel to be heroes?' calls our old friend Wanda Write-a-lot while Jimmy Snapshot clicks away with his camera.

'Pretty good, actually!' says Terry. Then he turns to us. 'Did you hear that? We're *heroes*. I've always wanted to be a hero.'

'Well,' I say, 'technically, it's me and Jill and everybody else who helped push who are the heroes, not you.'

'What do you mean?' says Terry.

'You're the one who left the door open,' I remind him. 'So you're really the villain.'

'No I'm not,' says Terry. 'Because nobody would be a hero if I hadn't left the door open in the first place. So really, I'm a double hero.'

'Speaking of doors, there's somebody at ours!' I say.

'It's probably the mayor come to pin our hero medals on us,' says Terry. 'I'd better go answer it.'

'I'll come, too,' says Jill.

'Last one there is a rotten egg,' I say, running ahead.

We open the door to see a man in a suit holding
a clipboard.

'Are you Andy, Terry and Jill?' he says.

'We sure are,' I say.

'We just saved everybody from all the weather,'
says Terry. 'We're heroes!'

'Yes, I know,' says the man. 'I saw you on TV—
which is why I'm here. My name is Mr Bunkoff.
I'm a school truancy officer. I thought I knew all
the eligible school-age students in the forest, but
I can't seem to find any record of you three on the
school rolls.'

'Oh, we're not students,' I say. 'We're treehouse builders and book-makers.'

'That doesn't matter,' says Mr Bunkoff. 'The law says everyone of school age must attend school … or else!'

'Or else what?' says Terry.

'Or else risk not being able to read or write,' he says.

'But we already know how to read and write,' says Terry. 'And we've already been to school. We went to Jill's early learning centre for animals.'

'Hmmm,' says Mr Bunkoff. 'That sounds rather unconventional. I'm talking about a proper school with qualified teachers, classrooms, a timetable and lots of learning opportunities and educational outcomes.'

'That sounds interesting,' says Jill. 'I've never been to school because I was too busy sailing around the world with my parents in our luxury superyacht.'

'I've never been either,' says Terry. 'My parents said it was too dangerous.'

'Oh, it's not dangerous at all!' says Mr Bunkoff with a laugh. 'And there's a big playground you can play in at little lunch and big lunch.'

'Little lunch *and* big lunch?' says Terry. 'Sign me up!'

'Me, too!' says Jill.

'Not me,' I say. 'I don't care how big the playground is or how many lunches there are: I don't want to go to school every day for the rest of my life.'

'*Every day?*' says Jill. 'For the rest of our *lives*? But what about my animals?'

'And what about our treehouse?' says Terry.

'Exactly!' I say.

'Don't worry,' says Mr Bunkoff. 'You only have to go to school from Monday to Friday. And not for the rest of your lives—just until you grow up.'

'I'm not sure I *want* to grow up,' says Terry.

'I'm afraid that will happen whether you want it to or not,' says Mr Bunkoff. 'It's just one of the many facts of life you'll learn when you go to school.'

'I'm not going to school!' I say. 'And neither are Terry and Jill.'

'Well,' says Mr Bunkoff, 'another fact of life you need to learn is that if you won't come willingly, then I'm authorised to take you by force.'

'You'll have to catch us first,' I say, slamming the door shut.

'**OPEN UP!**' Mr Bunkoff shouts angrily from the other side. 'OPEN UP OR ELSE!'

'Quick—run!' I say.

'Where to?' says Terry.

'The elevator!' I say.

We pile into the elevator and I push a whole bunch of buttons. I don't care where we're going as long as it's somewhere that Mr Bunkoff isn't.

'Phew, that was close!' I say as the elevator doors close. 'We almost ended up in *school*!'

CHAPTER 4

HALL OF FUNHOUSE MIRRORS

My stomach drops as we are whooshed up, up and away.

The elevator stops and the doors open. There are mirrors as far as we can see.

'I didn't know you had a mirror level,' says Jill.

'It's new,' I say. 'And even better, they're *funhouse* mirrors. It will be the perfect place to hide from Mr Bunkoff *and* have fun until the coast is clear.'

'Hey, look at me!' says Jill.

75

'Why is this one all covered up?' says Terry, standing next to a tall mirror that has a big red blanket over it.

DO NOT REMOVE THIS COVER by order of Andy

'Because it's a doppelganger mirror,' I say.
'I bought it from a travelling mirror salesman who told me it was dangerous and that I should never look into it.'

'Why would you buy a dangerous mirror that you can't look into?' says Jill.

'Because it was a really good deal,' I say. 'Such a good deal, in fact, *he* paid *me* to take it. Mirror deals don't get any better than that.'

'What's a doppelganger mirror?' says Terry.

'Beats me,' I say.

'Let's take the blanket off and find out,' says Terry.

'No, don't,' I say.

'What's the matter?' he says. 'Are you scared?'

'No,' I say. 'I just don't think it's a good idea.'

'Well, I *do*,' says Terry. 'So I'm taking it off!'

'I wouldn't if I were you,' I say.

'But you're *not* me,' says Terry. '*I'm* me and you're *you*.'

He takes hold of the blanket and says,

**'Mirror, mirror, on the wall,
who's the bravest one of all?'**

Then before I can stop him, he pulls it off with a flourish, covering us all in a cloud of dust.

When the dust clears we find ourselves staring at three weird reflections of ourselves. They're kind of *us* and *not-us* at the same time.

'What are *you* looking at, pal?' says my reflection.

'You,' I say. 'I mean *me*.'

'I ain't *you*,' says my reflection, 'and you definitely ain't *me*.'

'But if you're not me and I'm not you … then who *are* you, and what are you doing in the mirror?' I say.

'We're your doppelgangers, you dope!' he says. 'What did ya expect to see when you looked into a doppelganger mirror?'

'We weren't quite sure,' I admit. 'In fact, we didn't even know what a doppelganger was.'

'Well, now you do,' he says. 'I'm Anti-Andy and this is the rest of my gang, Terrible-Terry and Junkyard-Jill. But you can call us Anti-A, Terrible-T and Junkyard-J for short.'

'Pleased to meet you, Terrible-T,' says Terry.

'*Not* pleased to meet you,' says Terrible-T.

'That's not very nice,' says Terry.

'Well, we ain't nice,' says Terrible-T. 'We're doppelgangers—your evil twins—geddit?'

'Oh,' says Terry. 'So *that's* why we shouldn't have pulled the cover off!'

'He gets it,' says Junkyard-J. 'Finally!'

GROWL

'Why do they call you *Junkyard*-Jill?' says Jill.

'Because it's my name,' says Junkyard-J. 'And I run a junkyard. I *love* junk!'

'I love animals,' says Jill. 'Do you have any pets?'

'Just two junkyard dogs,' says Junkyard-J. 'But I wouldn't call them pets. Their names are Bitey One and Bitey Two, and if anyone tries to steal my junk, Biteys One and Two will bite their stealin' heads off!'

'Relax,' I say. 'We don't want to steal *your* junk. We've got plenty of our own. We've even got our own garbage dump.'

'Yeah,' says Terry. 'And it's got a magic wardrobe on top. You can read about it in our books.'

'We don't read books,' says Anti-A. 'Books are for chumps.'

'You're wrong about that,' I say. 'Books are for everyone. What even *is* a chump anyway?'

'You,' says Anti-A. '*You're* a chump.'

word-o-matic

chump
definition : a person who is easily tricked; a silly or foolish person, e.g. Andy.

'If you're not here to steal our junk, then why *are* you here?' says Junkyard-J.

'We're hiding from the truancy officer,' I say. 'He wants to take us to school but we don't want to go.'

'School's for fools,' says Anti-A.

'Well, at least we can agree on that,' I say. 'Maybe I'm not such a chump after all.'

'Yes, you are,' says Anti-A. 'We might agree on schools ... but you're still a chump.'

'That doesn't make any sense,' I say.

'Exactly what I'd expect a chump like you to say,' he says.

'Stop calling me a chump,' I say.

'Why don't you come into the mirror and *make* me?' says Anti-A.

'Don't do it, Andy!' says Jill. 'It might be a trick!'

'What's the matter?' says Junkyard-J. 'Scared of a little rumble, are ya?'

'Not at all,' says Jill. 'I'm pretty much the bravest person I know.'

'Oh yeah?' says Junkyard-J. 'Even braver than me?'

'Yeah!' says Jill.

'Why don't you come into the mirror and prove it then?' says Junkyard-J.

'Don't do it!' says Terry, stepping in front of Jill. 'It might be a trick!'

'Stay out of it,' says Terrible-T. 'Actually, on second thoughts, why don't *you* come into the mirror, too? The more the mirrorier—so, what are you waiting for? Come on in!'

'All right then, I will,' says Terry, stepping into the mirror.

'Wait, Terry,' I say, grabbing his arm to try to stop him.

But the mirror gang have hold of Terry's other arm and are pulling him their way.

Jill grabs Terry's arm and helps me pull him *our* way.

It's a tug of war and Terry's the rope!

'Aaarggh!' shouts Terry. 'You're tearing me apart!'

'Sorry,' says Jill. 'But it's for your own good. Pull harder, Andy—we're losing him!'

We pull
HARDER...

and
HARDER...

and

HARDER...

and just when we think
we can't possibly pull any

HARDER...

Terry comes flying back out of the mirror … with
Anti-A, Terrible-T and Junkyard-J as well!

CHAPTER 5

ALL TIED UP

Anti-A jumps to his feet.

'Ha-ha!' he cries. 'Our trick worked!'

'Yeah!' says Terrible-T. 'Let's go make some mirror-gang mischief!'

'Wait,' says Junkyard-J. 'What about the chumps?' She points at us. 'Maybe we should tie them up so they don't get in our way.'

'Good idea,' says Anti-A. 'Anybody got any rope?'

'No,' says Junkyard-J.

'Me neither,' says Terrible-T.

'I've got some,' says Terry, handing his doppelganger a large coil of rope.

'Thanks, pal,' sneers Terrible-T.

'Don't mention it,' says Terry. 'What are friends for?'

And before we know it, Jill and Terry and I are
bound tightly together.

'Terry!' I say. 'Why did you give him the rope?'

'I was just trying to be helpful,' says Terry.

'And you were,' says Terrible-T. 'Very, *very*
helpful!'

'All right, now let's go have some fun,' says Anti-A.
'Who's with me?'

'Me,' says Terrible-T.

'And me,' says Junkyard-J. 'All for one and one
for all, let's find some junk and have a ball!'

'SO LONG, SUCKERS,'

calls Anti-A as they run off, laughing.

The last thing we hear before the elevator doors slide shut is Terrible-T saying, 'I smell gingerbread—let's go eat it!'

'And I smell junk!' shouts Junkyard-J. 'Let's go grab it!'

'Well, this is just great, isn't it?' I say. 'The mirror gang are going to eat all our gingerbread and steal all our junk while we're stuck here tied up with rope that *you* gave them, Terry.'

'Look on the bright side, Andy,' says Terry. 'At least we're not at school!'

'And you do have a *lot* of gingerbread,' says Jill. 'And a lot of junk, for that matter! It's not like you'll miss any.'

'Are you kidding?' I say. 'All our junk is *essential*!'

'If it's essential, then it's not junk,' says Jill. 'So there's nothing to worry about.'

RING-RING!
RING-RING!
RING-RING!

'That sounds like the 3D video phone ringing,'
says Terry.

'That's because it *is* the 3D video phone
ringing,' I say. 'Thank goodness. We can ask
whoever it is to send help. Quick, answer it.'

103

'I can't,' says Terry. 'I'm tied up, remember?'

RING-RING!
RING-RING!
RING-RING!

'Oh, yeah,' I say. 'Me, too. Jill?'

'Sorry, all tied up,' she says. 'Let's hope it's Mr Big Nose and he answers the phone himself like he did before.'

RING-RING!
RING-RING!
RING-RING!

'Can't you chuckleheads answer your own phone?' says Mr Big Nose as his image flickers into focus on the screen. 'I'm busy enough answering my own calls without having to answer yours as well!'

Mosquito

'Sorry, Mr Big Nose,' I say. 'It's been a busy morning for us, too. After we got the weather dome door shut we had a visit from the truancy officer who wanted to make us all go to school, so we had to hide in the hall of mirrors and then Terry removed the cover from the doppelganger mirror and our doppelgangers got out and tied us all up and—'

'I'm going to stop you right there,' says Mr Big Nose. 'Save it for the book! The book you're supposed to deliver by five o'clock today or else!'

'And we will, I promise,' I say. 'But before we can do that we need to get untied, so if you could just reach through the screen and untie us that would be—'

'Request denied!' shouts Mr Big Nose. 'NMP!* Sort it out yourselves and make sure that book gets delivered by five. GoodBYE!'

The screen goes blank.

*Not My Problem!

'That was nice of him to call,' says Terry.

'It would have been nicer if he'd reached out of the screen and untied us,' I say.

'Shhh,' says Jill. 'Can you hear footsteps?'

'Yes!' says Terry. 'It's the mirror gang. They're coming back to untie us. I knew they would.'

'I'm not so sure about that,' says Jill. 'There's only one set of footsteps. I hope it's not who I think it is.'

'Me, too,' I say.

'Who are you both hoping it's not who you think it is?' says Terry.

'Mr Bunkoff,' I whisper. 'Shhh … be very quiet so he can't hear us.'

'TOO LATE!' says Mr Bunkoff as a big net comes down on top of us. 'GOTCHA!'

'Time for school,' he says.

'Please don't take us to school,' I beg.

'I have to,' says Mr Bunkoff as he carries us towards the elevator. 'It's the law.'

'But what about our book?' I say. 'We can't write the book if we're at school.'

'You don't need to worry about that,' says Mr Bunkoff. 'There are plenty of books where you're going!'

'Well, could you at least untie us first?' says Terry.

'Do I look like I came down in the last shower?' says Mr Bunkoff. 'I'll untie you when we get there and not a moment before!'

He
bundles
us into
the
elevator ...

pushes
the
ground
floor
button ...

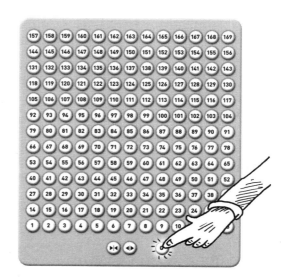

and the doors slide **SHUT** *!*

Uh-oh ... this is serious!

The elevator goes down and the doors open on the ground floor.

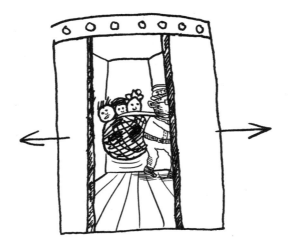

Mr Bunkoff loads us into the back of his van ...

drives us through the
forest …

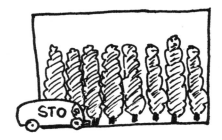

into the school …

up the stairs …

and dumps us
in a classroom.

CHAPTER 6

SHOW-AND-TELL

'Good morning, Ms Treacle,' says Mr Bunkoff.
'I've caught some new students for you.'

'Thank you, Mr Bunkoff,' says Ms Treacle.
'And welcome to you all. You're just in time for
show-and-tell. Why don't you start by telling us
a little about yourselves?'

'Well,' says Terry. 'My name is—'

'I'll handle this,' I say, interrupting him. 'I'm the narrator! My name is Andy, this is Terry, and this is Jill. We live in a 169-storey treehouse. Well, Jill doesn't live in the treehouse exactly, she lives in a cottage full of animals on the other side of the forest, but she hangs out with us a lot. We have a tank full of man-eating sharks and a bowling alley and an ice-cream parlour with 78 different flavours run by a robot called Edward Scooperhands—'

'What an interesting story!' says Ms Treacle, smiling. 'You obviously have a vivid imagination, Andy!'

'Well, maybe,' I say. 'But I'm not making this up. It's the truth. We really do live in a treehouse. You can read all about it in our books.'

'Oh, we don't have books like that in *our* school,' says Ms Treacle. 'Our principal, Mr Gradgrind, insists that we have only non-fiction in our library.'

'But our books *are* non-fiction,' I say.

'Excuse me, Ms Treacle,' says Terry. 'Incoming flying rabbit!'

'A flying *what*?' says Ms Treacle.

'RABBIT!' says Terry. 'Look out the window! There's a flying rabbit, and it's heading straight for us!'

I look up.
Terry's right—there really is a rabbit flying towards us, and it's coming fast!

Jill jumps up and opens the window just in time.

The rabbit flies through it and lands safely in her arms.

The class crowds around Jill, who
turns to Ms Treacle and says,
'Can this rabbit be my show-
and-tell?'

'I think it already is,' says
Ms Treacle, chuckling. 'I wonder
where it came from?'

'Just a moment,' says Jill.
'I'll ask it.' She holds the
rabbit up to her face,
twitches her nose and
makes a series of small
clicking noises.

The rabbit does
the same and soon
the two of them
are deep in
conversation.

'I hate to rush you, Jill,' says Ms Treacle, 'but we have to leave time for others to do their show-and-tell, too.'

'Sorry,' says Jill. 'Rabbits are very talkative—they can go on for hours. It says it was fired from the rocket-powered carrot-launcher in Andy and Terry's treehouse.'

'I think your imagination is every bit as good as Andy's!' says Ms Treacle.

'No, it's *true*!' says Jill. 'You see, this other Andy, Terry and Jill got out of the doppelganger mirror and they went to the carrot-launching level and launched this rabbit!'

Ahh!

BALI

7

'Those doppelganging fiends!' I say. 'They're going to wreck everything! Can we go home, please, Ms Treacle? We need to stop them before they do anything *really* bad.'

'I'm afraid not,' says Ms Treacle. 'School doesn't finish until three-thirty. Besides, it's time for Terry's show-and-tell.'

'Yay!' says Terry. 'Finally!'

'What do you have to show us today, Terry?' says Ms Treacle.

'Well,' says Terry, 'I, um, er … oh, I know! I can show you my lucky rubber band. I think I've got it here somewhere—ah, yes, here it is.'

Terry puts his hand in his pocket and pulls out what looks like a rubber band, but I can see it's not a rubber band. It's the rubber ring on the ripcord of his emergency inflatable underpants. But before I can warn him, the classroom is filled with a loud whooshing sound and his underpants have inflated to ten times their normal size.

'Oops!' says Terry.

Everybody laughs—well, everybody except
Ms Treacle.

'Settle down now,' she says, in a slightly louder
and slightly less sweet voice than before. 'That's
quite enough.'

'Sorry, Ms Treacle,' says Terry. 'It was an
accident. I'll just de-inflate them now.'

He fumbles for the de-inflating cord and pulls it.

As the air whooshes out of his underpants, Terry flies all arou

TERRY!

the classroom and bounces off the walls like a super ball.

This sets the class off laughing again and they don't stop until his pants get caught in the ceiling fan.

'Wheee!' says Terry, as he swings around and around above us. 'I'm flying!'

That's when there's a knock at the door.

KNOCK!
KNOCK!

CHAPTER 7

PRINCIPAL GRADGRIND

The door opens and a man wearing a military uniform marches into the room and glares at us.

Everybody in the class, including Ms Treacle, jumps to attention. (Well, everybody except Terry, who's still swinging from the ceiling fan.)

'Good morning, Principal Gradgrind,' says
Ms Treacle.

'GOOD?' he shouts. 'I don't see what's good
about it! I can hardly hear myself think above
all the noise coming from this classroom.'

'Well, you should think louder then,' says Terry.
'That's what I do when it gets too noisy in the
treehouse.'

'Who said that?'
says Principal
Gradgrind,
looking all
around him.

'I did!' says Terry. 'Up here!'

Principal Gradgrind looks up and sees Terry.
'What on earth are you doing up there?' he says.
'Get down at once!'

'I'd be happy to,' says Terry. 'But it's not that easy. My emergency inflatable underpants are stuck in the fan.'

'Then I'd advise you to get them unstuck as fast as possible!' says Principal Gradgrind.

'I'll try,' says Terry. He pulls and tugs at his underpants. There's a loud ripping noise and then he falls ...

and lands right on top of Principal Gradgrind!

'Get off me this instant!' says Principal Gradgrind, struggling to get out from underneath Terry.

I offer Terry my hand and pull him up.

Principal Gradgrind struggles to his feet and turns to face Ms Treacle.

'What is going on here?' he says. 'May I remind you this is a classroom, not a circus!'

'I'm very sorry, Principal Gradgrind,' says Ms Treacle. 'But, you see, we have some new students and they don't know all the rules yet.'

'Well, they'd better learn them, and fast!' says Principal Gradgrind, glaring at Terry and Jill and me. 'And one of the most important rules is NO SWINGING FROM THE CEILING FAN!'

'Why not?' says Terry.

'WHY NOT?' shouts Principal Gradgrind. 'Because it's a rule, that's why not! And speaking of rules, what's that rabbit doing in here? We have a strict no-animal policy, you know. No bringing animals of any kind to school, is that clear?'

'Yes, I suppose so,' says Jill. 'But I didn't *bring* the rabbit with me—it came flying in through the window. All I did was catch it.'

'Well, if you'd bothered learning the rules, you'd also know we have a strict no-catching policy as well,' says Principal Gradgrind. He unrolls a long piece of paper and starts reading: 'No catching balls! No catching colds! No catching trains! And above all, no catching rabbits! You three had better hurry up and learn the rules by three-thirty today ... OR ELSE!'

Principal Gradgrind rolls up his list of rules and stomps out of the room.

Everyone breathes a sigh of relief, including Ms Treacle.

'Is it time for our first lunch yet?' says Terry.

'Yes,' says Ms Treacle. 'Out you go.'

'YAY!' says Terry.

CHAPTER 8

TIME-OUT

We follow the other students out into the school yard.

'When do they give us our food?' says Terry.

'I don't know,' says Jill.

'I hope it's soon,' says Terry. 'It's been a long time since breakfast.'

'There's a tree full of apples over there,' I say.
'Let's climb up and pick some.'

'Last one up is a rotten apple,' says Terry.

'Wait for me,' says Jill.

'I wouldn't do that if I were you,' says one
of the students.

'Why not?' says Terry, who's already halfway
up the tree.

'Because climbing trees is against the rules,' says the student.

'But that's silly,' says Jill, swinging herself up into the tree with Terry. 'Climbing trees is fun!'

'And quite safe, too,' I say, joining them. 'You can't fall if you hang on. Who'd like an apple?'

'**Me! Me! Me!**' shout the students.

'Okay,' I say. 'Here they come!'

We pick apples and throw them down to the students waiting below.

'Uh-oh,' says one of the students. 'Here comes Principal Gradgrind.'

We watch as he strides angrily across the playground towards us.

'WHAT ARE YOU DOING UP THERE?' he shouts.

'Picking apples,' says Terry. 'Would you like one?'

'NO!' says Principal Gradgrind. 'WHAT I *WOULD* LIKE IS FOR YOU TO GET DOWN OUT OF THAT TREE THIS INSTANT!'

'But it's fun up here,' says Terry.

'I don't care how much fun it is,' says Principal
Gradgrind. 'Tree climbing is against school rules.'

'Then maybe you should change the rules,'
I suggest.

'Yeah,' says Terry. 'You should make it a rule that
everybody has to climb a tree every day. Why don't
you come up and see for yourself how nice it is?'

'I'VE GOT A BETTER IDEA,' says Principal
Gradgrind. 'WHY DON'T YOU COME DOWN
RIGHT NOW?!'

'Okay, you're the boss,' says Terry.

But before we can climb down there's a cracking
noise …

the branch we're sitting on breaks and we all
fall down …

and land right on top of Principal Gradgrind!

'RIGHT, THAT DOES IT!' says Principal
Gradgrind, crawling out from beneath us.

'Sorry, Principal Gradgrind,' I say. 'It was an
accident. It's not our fault the branch broke.'

'Of course it's your fault!' says Principal
Gradgrind. 'The branch wouldn't have broken
if you hadn't been sitting on it! You three can go
straight to the time-out room.'

'What's that?' says Terry. 'Is it something to do with time travel?'

'No, it most certainly is not,' says Principal Gradgrind. 'It's a room where students take time out to reflect on their actions. Follow me!'

We follow Principal Gradgrind to a door marked TIME-OUT.

'IN THERE, NOW!' he says, opening the door.

We walk in. There's an open window with bars across it, and the walls are bare except for a list of time-out room rules.

TIME-OUT ROOM

RULES

☒ NO talking

☒ NO singing

☒ NO dancing

☒ NO removing the piece of paper these rules are written on, writing an SOS message on the back, folding it into a paper plane and throwing it out the window ... OR ELSE!

BY ORDER OF PRINCIPAL GRADGRIND

'How long do we have to stay here?' says Terry.

'Until you can demonstrate to me that you are prepared to be cooperative and rule-abiding members of the school community,' says Principal Gradgrind.

He leaves the room, shutting the door behind him.

After about a minute, Terry says, 'I think I'm feeling much more cooperative and rule-abiding now. How about you guys?'

'Yeah,' I say. 'I'm ready to leave.'

'So am I,' says Jill. 'Let's go.'

I try to open the door … but the handle won't budge.

'It's locked,' I say. 'There's no way out!'

'Then it should be called a time-IN room,' says Terry.

'Maybe you were right about school, Andy,' says Jill. 'I don't think it's quite as much fun as Mr Bunkoff made it out to be, and their anti-animal policy is very harsh.'

'Yeah,' says Terry. 'There are way too many rules.'

'Hmm ... rules,' I say. 'That gives me an idea—this list is written on paper. I could write a message on the back and then fold it into a paper plane and throw it out the window.'

'But that's exactly what the time-out room rules say you're not allowed to do,' says Jill.

'I know,' I say. 'But this is an *emergency*. I'm sure Principal Gradgrind will understand. I just need something to write with. Do you have your spooncil handy, Terry?'

'Yes, but it's up my nose,' he says. 'You'll have to make me sneeze to get it out.'

'Ugh,' says Jill. 'You can borrow my forkcil if you like.'

'What's a forkcil?' I say.

'It's just like a spooncil,' says Jill. 'Except that the spoon bit is a fork. And I don't keep it up my nose.'

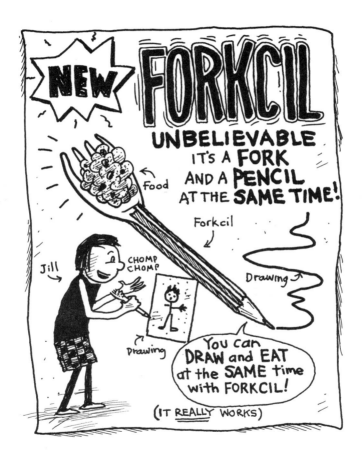

Jill takes it out of her ear and hands it to me.

'Thanks,' I say, and I start writing.

Dear whoever finds this note,

How are you?
That's great to hear!
We're fine, too. Well, when
I say 'fine', I don't mean
FINE fine—I mean not too
fine at all really because we're
trapped in the time-out room
and we need you to come and
rescue us immediately, please.

Thanks in advance,
Andy, Terry & Jill

Then I fold the sheet of paper into a super-fast paper plane,

and throw it out the window.

'So what do we do now?' says Terry.

'We wait until somebody finds our message and comes to let us out!' I say.

'Waiting, waiting, waiting, waiting ...' says Terry.

'What are you doing?' I say.

'Waiting,' he says. 'Just like you told me.'

'Well, could you wait a bit quieter, please?'

'Of course,' whispers Terry. 'Waiting, waiting, waiting, waiting, waiting, waiting, waiting, waiting, waiting, waiting ...'

CHAPTER 9

TIME-IN

Suddenly the door opens and Principal Gradgrind walks in, holding a paper plane in his hand.

'Gee, that was quick,' says Terry. 'Thanks for coming to rescue us!'

'I haven't come to rescue you,' he says. 'I've come to find out why you removed the time-out rules from the wall, wrote a message on the back, folded it into a paper plane and threw it out the window, despite the rules specifically forbidding such actions!'

'Because it was an emergency,' says Terry. 'But where did you find it?'

'In the garden beneath the window,' says Principal Gradgrind. 'Do you have anything to say for yourselves?'

'Yes,' I say. 'It must have been a bad throw. Can I try again, please?'

'No, you may not!' he says. 'But you *can* unfold the piece of paper, put it back up on the wall and memorise the rules and regulations written on it.'

'I've got a better idea,' I say. 'How about you just let us go back home to our treehouse and we'll never bother you or break any of your rules ever again?'

'I think you've already wasted quite enough time in that treehouse of yours,' says Principal Gradgrind.

'But we *don't* waste time!'* I say. 'Terry and I make books for Mr Big Nose and Jill runs an intergalactic animal rescue service.'

*Unless we're in the time-wasting level, of course.

'I also run a Ninja Snail Training Academy,' says Terry.

'That's ridiculous!' says Principal Gradgrind. 'I've never heard anything so nonsensical!'

'You obviously haven't heard our three wise owls,' I say. 'They're even nonsensicaller.'

'But very wise,' says Terry.

'I'm not so sure about that,' says Jill.

THE THREE WISE OWLS

I look up and see something flying through the bars of the window. 'Incoming UFO!' I shout.

'Don't be silly,' says Principal Gradgrind. 'There's no such thing as UFOs!'

'No, you don't understand,' I say. 'Not an *alien* UFO, an *Unidentified Flying Object* UFO—and it's heading straight for you. Stand clear!'

I duck but Principal Gradgrind doesn't. The UFO flies through the bars of the window and lodges itself firmly in his upper arm.

He looks at it, puzzled, and moves as if to pull it out, but then he closes his eyes and slumps to the ground.

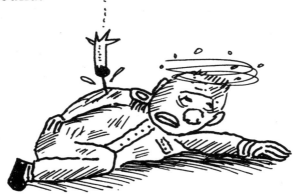

'Principal Gradgrind,' I say, kneeling beside him. 'Wake up!'

'It's no use,' says Jill. 'I don't think he's going to wake up.'

'You mean ... he's *d-d-dead*?' I say.

'No,' says Jill, pulling the UFO from Principal Gradgrind's arm and examining it. 'This isn't a UFO, it's an ATD—an Animal Tranquilliser Dart, and now he's full of animal tranquilliser. I'm guessing he'll be sleeping soundly for quite some time.'

'But who would want to tranquillise Principal Gradgrind?' I say.

'I think I know,' says Terry, looking out the window. 'And here they come.'

'Who?' I say.

'The mirror gang,' says Terry. 'And about a million monkeys.'

Jill and I look. Terry's right. Well, almost.

The mirror gang, and at least a *hundred* million monkeys, are headed straight for the school.

Anti-A's face appears at the window. 'I told you school was for chumps,' he says, 'and now look at ya! Lucky we're here to bust you out.'

'But how did you know where to find us?' I say.

'Well, we saw youse all gettin' carted off by that truancy officer chump and we figured this is where he brought ya!'

'Gee, but they sure got you banged up good and proper, ain't they?' says Junkyard-J, peering through the window. 'Bars and all! But that shouldn't be a problem. Not for someone as strong as me.'

She bends and snaps the bars until there is a gap
big enough for us to climb through.

'That's amazing!' says Jill. 'How'd you get so
strong?'

'Haulin' junk,' says Junkyard-J. 'Well, don't just
stand there gawkin', you lot. Get out while the
goin's good.'

We climb out through the window into the
playground, which is full of monkeys.

The monkeys are having a great time on the monkey bars (which makes sense I guess).

'Thanks for getting us out of there,' I say. 'But why are you here? And where did all the monkeys come from?'

'From the monkey house at the zoo,' says Terrible-T. 'They helped us escape.'

'You were in the *monkey house*?' I say.

'Yeah,' says Anti-A. 'It's a long story.'

'Ooh goody,' says Terry. 'I *love* long stories. Tell us all about it.'

'I'm not really a good narrator,' says Anti-A.

'Don't worry,' says Terry. 'Neither is Andy, and he does it all the time.'

'Hey!' I say.

'Be quiet,' says Jill. 'Let's hear the story.'

Well, after we tied you up we found a house made out of gingerbread, and a little old lady told us to eat as much as we liked, so we ate the whole house and then we ate her as well.

CHOMP

CHOMP

I said eat up, not eat ME up!

'You *ate* the gingerbread lady?' says Terry.

'Yeah,' says Terry-T. 'She tasted nice—she was made of gingerbread, too!'

'We know!' says Jill. 'It came flying through the classroom window and I caught it.'

'Oh, it's *so* cute!' says Junkyard-J, reaching out to pat it and then suddenly pulling her hand back. 'I mean, ahem, if you like that sort of thing.'

'I do,' says Jill. 'And so can *you*. You don't have to choose—you can like rabbits *and* junk.'

'Hey, quit interrupting my story,' says Anti-A. 'You wanna hear what happened next or not?'

'Yes,' says Jill. 'Go on.'

Well, then the 3D video phone started ringing and this chump with the biggest schnozz you've ever seen came on and he was like, 'Write my book OR ELSE!'

And I was like, 'We're not writing no dumb book,' and he went, 'Well then it's the monkey house for you until you do, and if you don't, then I'll bulldoze the treehouse and sell the parts for scrap and you can all stay in the monkey house forever and ever and ever!'

*And then he reached out of the screen,
grabbed us all in his big dirty mitt ...*

and slung us out of the tree.

and all the way to the zoo—where we landed in a dirty, rotten, stinkin' monkey house full of dirty, rotten, stinkin' monkeys!

'So, did you write the book?' says Jill.

'Nah!' says Anti-A. 'Of course not!'

'Then how did you get out?' I say.

'I'll tell you in the next chapter,' says Anti-A, wiping sweat off his brow. 'I need a break. This narratin' is hard work!'

'Tell me about it,' I say.

CHAPTER 10

MONKEY MAYHEM

So there we were sittin' in the monkey house surrounded by monkeys, and Terrible-T and Junkyard-J were like, 'What are we gonna do?' and I says to them, 'I'll tell ya what we're gonna do. We're gonna break out of this monkey house and then break those chumps out of school so they can write the book and we can go back to our mirror—that's what we're gonna do!'

And all the monkeys were like, 'Well if you're breaking out, then we're comin' with you!' And so I says, 'In that case, let's work together. I need you monkeys to make a monkey tower so we can climb up, and when we get to the top we'll pull you guys up after us.'

So they piled on top of each other into the tallest monkey tower you ever saw and we climbed up and out of there.

And once we—and all the monkeys—were out, the zookeepers were like, 'Stop right there or we'll fire our tranquilliser guns,' and I was like, 'We're not stoppin', no way, hose-ay!' And the next thing ya know, we're runnin' and tranquilliser darts are goin' everywhere.

'So that must be how Principal Gradgrind got the dart in his arm,' says Terry.

'Who's that?' says Anti-A.

'The school principal,' I say. 'The one who makes all the rules.'

'Rules—YECH!' says Anti-A.

'Don't worry,' I say. 'He won't be making any rules for quite some time. He's been tranquillised.'

'Hey, where have all the monkeys gone?' says Jill.

I look around. The playground is empty—well, apart from us, that is.

'Uh-oh,' says Terry. 'Look at the school— it's monkey mayhem!'

'This is not just monkey mayhem,' I say. 'This is MEGA monkey mayhem!'

'Oh dear,' says Jill, using her emergency bird-watching binoculars to look into the classrooms. 'This isn't just regular MEGA monkey mayhem—this is MASSIVE mega monkey mayhem! The monkeys are in the science room. If they're not careful, they're going to blow up the whole school. Take cover!'

VIEW INSIDE THE SCIENCE ROOM FROM JILL'S

EMERGENCY BIRD-WATCHING BINOCULARS

And sure enough …

185

'Uh-oh,' I say. 'Principal Gradgrind is not going to like this—I'm pretty sure blowing up the school is against the rules.'

CHAPTER 11

THE 13-STOREY TREEHOUSE SCHOOL

I look around. There's nothing but a pile of broken bricks, splintered wood, destroyed desks and wrecked whiteboards where the school used to be.

'Our school!' cries Ms Treacle, emerging from the wreckage. 'What happened to our lovely school?'

'Monkeys,' says Terry.

'But where did they come from?' says Ms Treacle.

'They followed the mirror gang here,' says Jill.

'The mirror gang?' says Ms Treacle.

'That's us,' says Anti-A, stepping forward. 'Me and my pals Terrible-Terry and Junkyard-Jill. Sorry about your school, but look on the bright side—now you don't *have* a school.'

'But I liked school,' says Ms Treacle.

'Don't be a chump,' says Anti-A. '*Nobody* likes school.'

'*We* did,' say the students.

'And so did Principal Gradgrind,' says Ms Treacle. 'And speaking of Principal Gradgrind, where is he?'

'Last time we saw him he was in the time-out room,' I say.

'We'd better go look for him,' says Jill. 'He might be hurt. Come on.'

I'm searching around near where the time-out
room used to be when I hear loud snoring.

The snoring is coming from under a big sheet
of metal. I lift it up and there is Principal
Gradgrind, safe and sound, sleeping like
a baby. Except that babies, as far as
I know, don't snore quite
so loudly.

Disturbed by the light, Principal Gradgrind wakes up.

'What happened?' he says. 'Where's the time-out room gone? And where's my school, for that matter?'

'It's destroyed,' says Ms Treacle.

'Destroyed?' says Principal Gradgrind.

'Yes—and it's all *their* fault,' says Ms Treacle, pointing at us.

'It's not *our* fault,' I say. 'The monkeys did it!'

'Well, I can't expel monkeys,' says Principal Gradgrind. 'But I can expel *you*. You are all hereby officially expelled from this school … forever!'

'We wasn't even enrolled in the first place,' says Anti-A. 'And what school are you even talkin' about? I don't see no school around here.'

'I'm referring to the school that *was* here,' says Principal Gradgrind. 'The school that was my life! What am I going to do now?'

'How about you give everyone the rest of the day off?' suggests Terrible-T.

'No, I've got an even better idea,' says Anti-A. 'How about you give everyone the rest of their *lives* off?'

'Not a chance,' says Principal Gradgrind. 'I built this school with nothing but the sweat of my brow and an instruction book called *How to Build a School With Nothing but the Sweat of Your Brow and This Book* and I can—and will—do it again! Who's going to help me?'

'**ME!**' says Ms Treacle.

'**ME!**' say the students.

'**ME!**' says Terry.

'**AND ME!**' says Jill.

'What are you saying?' I whisper to Jill and Terry. 'We're expelled! We can go home now ... and you want to *rebuild* the school?'

'I know it wasn't perfect,' says Jill. 'But it definitely had potential—and it's *fun* to learn new things. Plus, I feel bad that the school got wrecked.'

'But that wasn't *our* fault,' I say. 'It was the monkeys!'

'I know,' says Jill. 'But I can't help feeling a little bit responsible all the same.'

'And it's fun building stuff, Andy!' says Terry. 'We do it all the time, remember?'

'That's true,' I say. 'And I guess it could be fun building a school if we add a few interesting features, like a giant water slide and a secret underground science lab.'

'And a rabbit sanctuary!' says Jill.

'And let's make it that they have three lunches!' says Terry. 'A little one, a big one, and a *really* big one!'

'Okay,' I say. 'Count me in.'

'And count us OUT!' says Anti-A.

'But none of this would have happened if you hadn't tricked us into pulling you out of the doppelganger mirror,' I say. 'The least you can do is help us.'

'Wrong,' says Anti-A. 'The least we can do is nuthin'—and that's exactly what *we* intend to do. Nuthin'!'

'Nuthin', nuthin', nuthin'!' chime in Terrible-T and Junkyard-J. 'Nuthin', nuthin', nuthin'!'

'Have it your way,' says Jill. 'But we're going to help rebuild the school, and the more people who help, the faster it will be built and the sooner we'll get home. And the sooner we get home, the sooner Andy and Terry can get their book done and you can go back to your mirror.'

'Well,' says Junkyard-J, 'if you put it like that, maybe I can help a *little* bit, and do sumthin'.'

'Yeah,' says Terrible-T. 'If it gets us home faster, then I might as well do sumthin', too.'

'That's the spirit,' I say. 'So, Anti-A, what do you say? Will you help?'

Anti-A shrugs. 'I'll never understand you non-mirror chumps,' he says. 'You've got everything back to front. But yeah, okay, whatevs.'

'What are we all waiting for?' I say. 'Let's get building!'

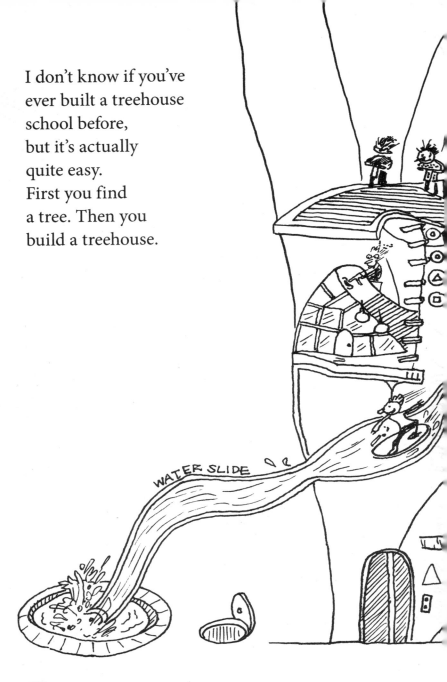

I don't know if you've
ever built a treehouse
school before,
but it's actually
quite easy.
First you find
a tree. Then you
build a treehouse.

WATER SLIDE

Then you add some classrooms.

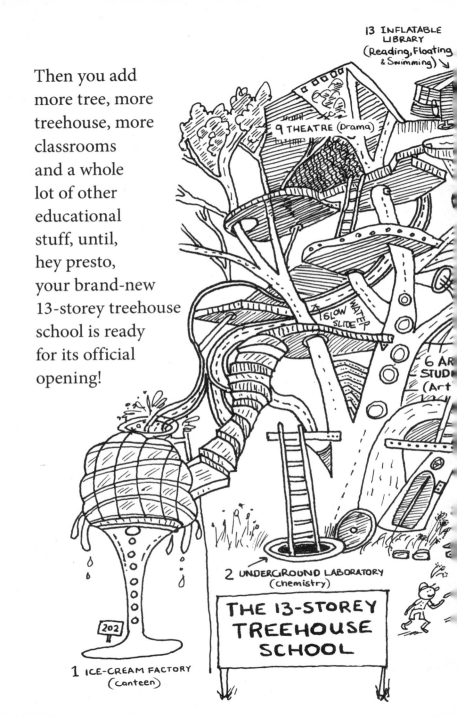

Then you add more tree, more treehouse, more classrooms and a whole lot of other educational stuff, until, hey presto, your brand-new 13-storey treehouse school is ready for its official opening!

13 INFLATABLE LIBRARY (Reading, Floating & Swimming)

9 THEATRE (Drama)

6 SLOW WATER SLIDE

6 ART STUDI (Art

2 UNDERGROUND LABORATORY (chemistry)

THE 13-STOREY TREEHOUSE SCHOOL

202

1 ICE-CREAM FACTORY (canteen)

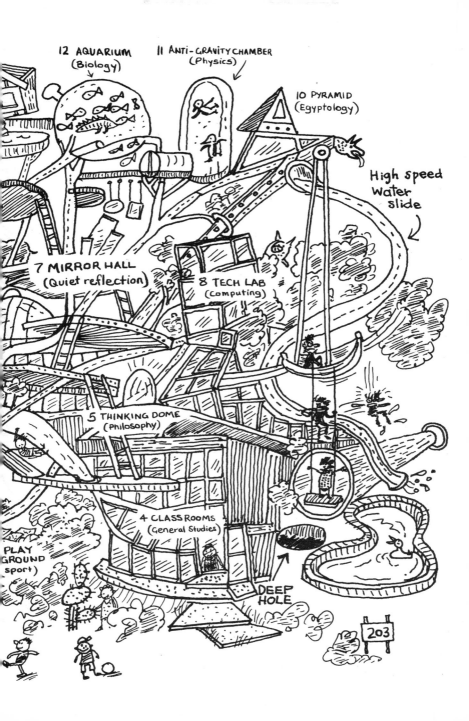

'I now declare The 13-Storey Treehouse School open!'
says Principal Gradgrind,
cutting the ribbon.

We all cheer.

'It's the greatest school ever,' says Principal Gradgrind. 'Even better than the old one—and that was already the greatest school in the world.'

'Even *I* wouldn't mind going to a school like this,' I say.

'Me neither,' says Anti-A.

'Or me,' says Terrible-T.

'Or me,' says Junkyard-J.

'I'm afraid that's not going to be possible,' says Principal Gradgrind.

'Why not?' says Anti-A. 'Is it because we're from a mirror?'

'No,' says Principal Gradgrind. 'It's because, after seeing your incredible building and leadership skills here today, I realise there's nothing we can teach you that you don't already know. You can all consider yourselves the first graduates of The 13-Storey Treehouse School. Here are your certificates.'

'Thanks,' I say. 'These are going straight to the trophy room. Now, if you'll excuse us, we've got a book to write.'

'Can we help you write the book?' says Anti-A as we head back to the treehouse. 'Tellin' that story before was fun.'

'Of course,' I say. 'The more the merrier—and I think you've definitely got the knack for it.'

'And can we be in it?' says Terrible-T.

'You sure can,' says Terry. 'We're going to write about everything that's happened today and everyone we've met—and that includes you.'

'And Bitey One and Bitey Two as well?' says Junkyard-J.

'You betcha!' says Jill.

THERE'S NO HOME LIKE A TREEHOUSE

We go back home and start writing—and drawing—the book.

We write.

Well, when I say 'tree', I mean treehouse. And when I say 'treehouse', I don't just mean any old treehouse—I mean a *169-storey* treehouse. (It used to be a 156-storey treehouse, but we've added another 13 storeys.)

So what are you waiting for? Come on up!

CHUTNEY!

BARK

BARK!

GIANT RABBIT

REPORT

SECRET LABORATORY

4

5

We draw.

Oh, great—the wind just blew all the blankets off my bed. This is the most unrelaxing Monday morning sleep-in ever!

HOWL!

And then it gets even more unrelaxing when, with a loud WHUMP and a high-pitched EEK, Jill lands on my bed!

'Jill?' I say. 'What are you doing here?'

WHUMP!

EEK!

'I don't know!' she says. 'One moment I was having a lovely indoor picnic with my animals, then the next thing I knew, there was this huge storm and it blew my cottage away. And then it blew me away as well and I landed here!'

34

35

BLAH! BLAH!

We draw.

We write.

FLYING PIG
↑
words

← picture

We write and write and write.

'I can't,' says Terry. 'I'm tied up, remember?'

RING-RING!
RING-RING!
RING-RING!

'Oh, yeah,' I say. 'Me, too. Jill?'

RING-RING!
RING-RING!
RING-RING!

'Sorry, all tied up,' she says. 'Let's hope it's Mr Big Nose and he answers the phone himself like he did before.'

RING-RING!
RING-RING!
RING-RING!

104   105

We draw and draw and draw.

As the air whooshes out of his underpants, Terry flies all around the classroom and bounces off the walls like a super ball.

TERRY!

That's good

SPELLING!

OOPS!

126   127

210

We write and draw and draw and write.

'Why not?' says Terry.

'WHY NOT?' shouts Principal Gradgrind. 'Because it's a rule, that's why not! And speaking of rules, what's that rabbit doing in here? We have a strict no-animal policy, you know. No bringing animals of any kind to school, is that clear?'

'Yes, I suppose so,' says Jill. 'But I didn't *bring* the rabbit with me—it came flying in through the window. All I did was catch it.'

'Well, if you'd bothered learning the rules, you'd also know we have a strict no-catching policy as well,' says Principal Gradgrind. He unrolls a long piece of paper and starts reading: 'No catching balls! No catching colds! No catching trains! And above all, no catching rabbits! You three had better hurry up and learn the rules by three-thirty today … OR ELSE!'

134

We draw and write and write and draw.

'There's a tree full of apples over there,' I say. 'Let's climb up and pick some.'

'Last one up is a rotten apple,' says Terry.

'Wait for me,' says Jill.

'I wouldn't do that if I were you,' says one of the students.

'Why not?' says Terry, who's already halfway up the tree.

138

'Because climbing trees is against the rules,' says the student.

'But that's silly,' says Jill, swinging herself up into the tree with Terry. 'Climbing trees is fun!'

'And quite safe, too,' I say, joining them. 'You can't fall if you hang on. Who'd like an apple?'

'Me! Me! Me!' shout the students.

'Okay,' I say. 'Here they come!'

We pick apples and throw them down to the students waiting below.

139

We write, write, write.

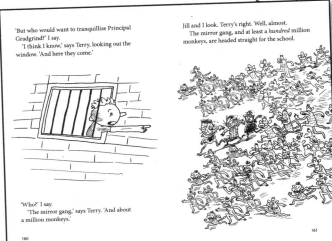

'But who would want to tranquillise Principal Gradgrind?' I say.

'I think I know,' says Terry, looking out the window. 'And here they come.'

'Who?' I say.

'The mirror gang,' says Terry. 'And about a million monkeys.'

160

Jill and I look. Terry's right. Well, almost.

The mirror gang, and at least a *hundred* million monkeys, are headed straight for the school.

161

We draw, draw, draw.

WRITE!

GLOOP!

J

'Oh dear,' says Jill, using her emergency bird-watching binoculars to look into the classrooms. 'This isn't just regular MEGA monkey mayhem—this is MASSIVE mega monkey mayhem! The monkeys are in the science room. If they're not careful, they're going to blow up the whole school. Take cover!'

VIEW INSIDE THE SCIENCE ROOM FROM JILL'S   EMERGENCY BIRD-WATCHING BINOCULARS

182   183

GIANT RABBIT

picture → 🐒 ← SMALL FLEA ← words → GIANT RABBIT

We write and draw and write.

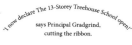

'I now declare The 13-Storey Treehouse School open!' says Principal Gradgrind, cutting the ribbon.

We all cheer.

'It's the greatest school ever,' says Principal Gradgrind. 'Even better than the old one—and that was already the greatest school in the world.'

'Even *I* wouldn't mind going to a school like this,' I say.

'Me neither,' says Anti-A.

'Or me,' says Terrible-T.

'Or me,' says Junkyard-J.

'I'm afraid that's not going to be possible,' says Principal Gradgrind.

'Why not?' says Anti-A. 'Is it because we're from a mirror?'

'No,' says Principal Gradgrind. 'It's because, after seeing your incredible building and leadership skills here today, I realise there's nothing we can teach you that you don't already know. You can all consider yourselves the first graduates of The 13-Storey Treehouse School. Here are your certificates.'

'Thanks,' I say. 'These are going straight to the trophy room. Now, if you'll excuse us, we've got a book to write.'

We draw and write and draw.

'Can we help you write the book?' says Anti-A as we head back to the treehouse. 'Tellin' that story before was fun.'

'Of course,' I say. 'The more the merrier—and I think you've definitely got the knack for it.'

'And can we be in it?' says Terrible-T.

'You sure can,' says Terry. 'We're going to write about everything that's happened today and everyone we've met—and that includes you.'

'And Bitey One and Bitey Two as well?' says Junkyard-J.

'You betcha!' says Jill.

CHAPTER 12

THERE'S NO HOME LIKE A TREEHOUSE

We go back home and start writing—and drawing—the book.

Until we're all finished!

Until we're all finished!

'Hey, making books is even more fun than I thought it would be,' says Anti-A.

'Yeah, but we're not quite finished yet,' I say. 'We have to get it to Mr Big Nose and we don't have much time.'

'I've got an idea,' says Terry, 'let's send it by tornado! I'll just let a *little* one out of the weather dome and we'll put the book in it and give it a push towards Mr Big Nose's office.'

214

215

'Hey, making books is even more fun than I thought it would be,' says Anti-A.

'Yeah, but we're not quite finished yet,' I say. 'We have to get it to Mr Big Nose and we don't have much time.'

'I've got an idea,' says Terry, 'let's send it by tornado! I'll just let a *little* one out of the weather dome and we'll put the book in it and give it a push towards Mr Big Nose's office.'

'I don't know if that's such a good idea,' says Jill. 'There's no telling what sort of damage a tornado might do—even a little one.'

'Jill's right,' I say. 'A tornado is not the answer.'

'But there's no other possible way to do it in time,' says Terry.

'Yes there is,' I say. 'You're forgetting we have a world class paper plane research and development facility. All we have to do is make a paper plane capable of flying faster than the speed of sound and then we'll attach the book to it.'

'A supersonic paper plane?' says Terry. 'Are you for real? Is such a thing even possible?'

'Sure,' I say. 'Some people look at things the way they are and say "Why?" But I dream of things that never were and say "Why not?"'

'But what about the last super-fast plane you made?' says Jill. 'No offence, but it wasn't very good. It barely even made it out the window before it crashed.'

'There was nothing wrong with the plane,' I say.
'It was just a bad throw. But we've got Junkyard-J
to throw this one for us. She's strong enough to
give it the extra thrust it needs to break the sound
barrier and get our book delivered on time. Come
on, let's go!'

We hotfoot it to the paper plane research and
development facility to research, develop and
build the world's first supersonic paper
plane in record time.

PPRDF

Finally it's ready for take-off—or, in this case, Junkyard-J-off. She launches it from the top of the treehouse with a mighty throw.

It flies up into the sky ...

Unicorn noise

and over the city to Big Nose Books.

'Well, that all worked out okay,' says Terry. 'What will we do now?'

'I reckon we'd better be gettin' back home to our mirror,' says Anti-A.

'Yeah, I sure have missed it,' says Terrible-T. 'You should come and visit us some time.'

'We will,' I say. 'And if you have any improvements you'd like to make, we'd be happy to help you with them.'

'Thanks,' says Terrible-T. 'That carrot-launcher was a lot of fun. I wouldn't mind one of my own.'

'I can help you build a nice cosy kennel for Bitey One and Bitey Two,' says Jill.

'I reckon they'd like that—and so would I,' says Junkyard-J, as she steps back into the mirror. 'I'll go and tell the Biteys the good news.'

'I guess I'll see you chumps later,' says Anti-A, grinning as he follows Junkyard-J into the mirror.

'It's been nice visiting you,' says Terrible-T, waving goodbye. 'But as much fun as it's been, it's good to be home.'

'I agree with Terrible-T,' says Terry. 'It *is* good to be home again.'

'Oh dear,' says Jill. 'That reminds me—I don't have a home any more. My cottage was blown away in the storm.'

Terry and I look at each other.

I can tell he's thinking exactly the same thing as me.

'Hey, Jill,' I say. 'Why don't you and your animals come and live in the treehouse with us? We can build you a cottage on our spare 169th storey.'

'Yeah,' says Terry. 'What do you think, Jill?'

'Oh my goodness,' says Jill. 'That would be amazing—I would love it! And so would my animals! Yes please!'

'Yay!' says Terry. 'Let's get started right away.'

CHAPTER 13

THE LAST CHAPTER

Given that we've already built a 169-storey treehouse, a treehouse school *and* a supersonic paper plane, building a single-storey cottage exactly like Jill's old one is easy and doesn't take us very long at all.

'It's *perfect*,' says Jill. 'And the view from up here is spectacular! Now all I have to do is to move my animals in … Uh-oh …'

'What's the matter?' I say.

'I'm not sure where my animals are—I haven't seen them since the wind blew them and my cottage away.'

'Don't worry,' says Terry. 'The GRABINATOR can find them all and bring them to their new home.'

So Terry fires up the GRABINATOR and starts to grab.

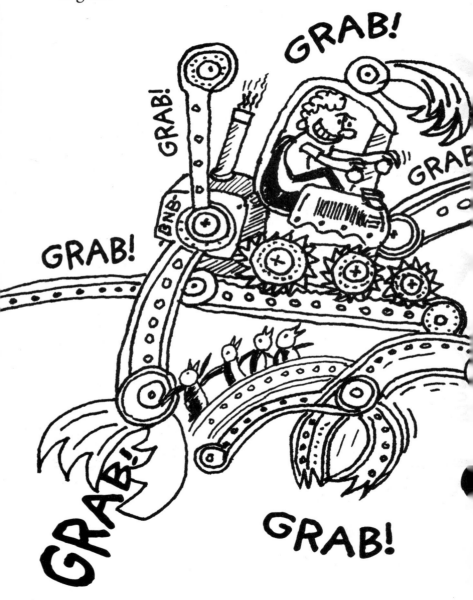

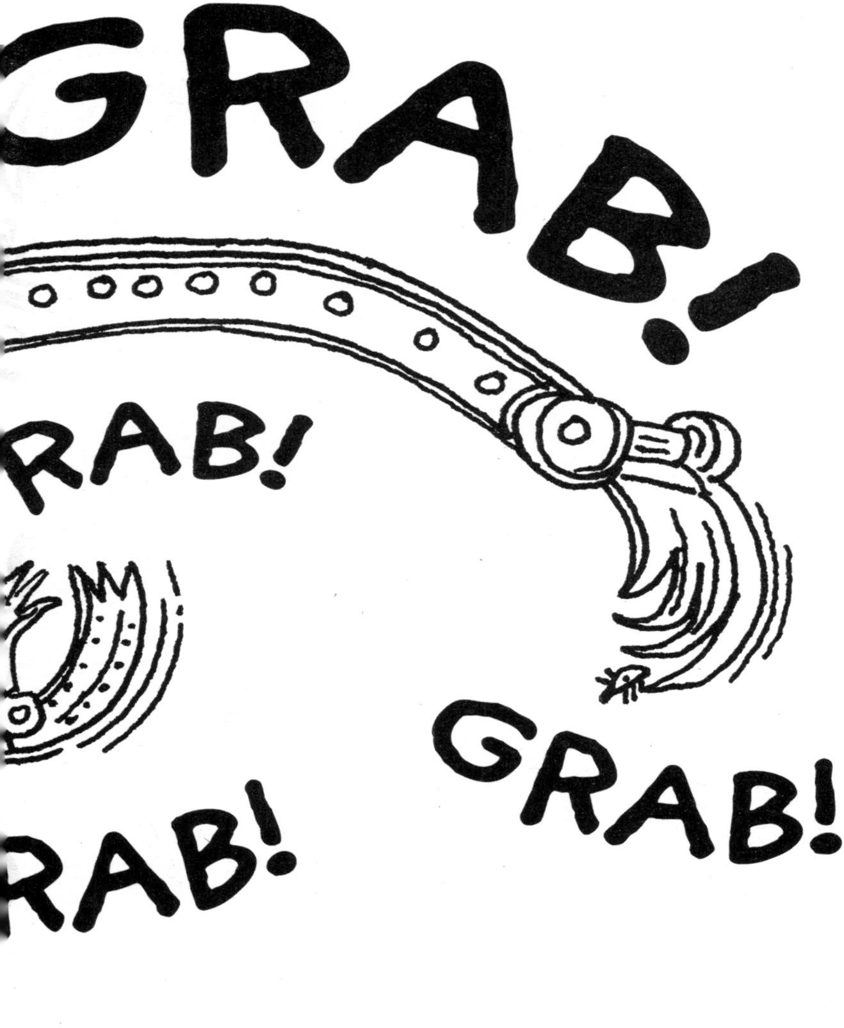
GRAB!
RAB!
GRAB!
RAB!

He grabs and grabs and grabs and grabs and grabs and grabs and grabs and grabs and grabs until all of Jill's animals (and a few others that aren't Jill's

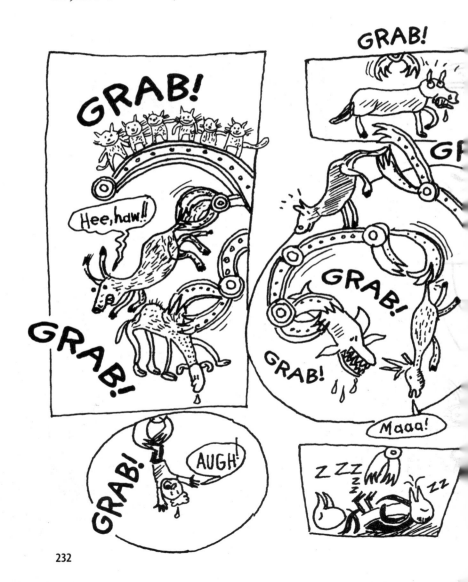

but don't seem to mind too much) have been grabbed and placed in their new home.

'It's so nice to see you all again,' says Jill. 'I've missed you.'

'Hee, haw!' says Mr Hee-Haw.

'You're right about that,' says Jill.

'What did he say?' says Terry.

'He said there's no place like home,' says Jill.

'Exactly!' says Terry. 'And there's no home like a treehouse.'

'You can say that again,' I say.

'There's no home like a treehouse,' says Terry.
'There's no home like a treehouse … there's no
home like a treehouse … there's no home like a—'

'You can stop saying it now,' I say.

'Why?' says Terry.

'Because it's the end of the book,' I say.

'Wait,' says Terry. 'Can we have a zoom-out ending? We've never done that before.'

'Sure!' I say.

'Yay!' says Terry.

'Double yay,' says Jill. 'I love zoom-out endings!'

'Okay then,' I say. 'One zoom-out ending coming up. Everybody hold on tight. That goes for you, too, readers. Here we go!'

MOO!

239

Cloud →

Treehouse

THE END

Lots of laughs

at every level!

Lots of laughs

at every level!

ANDY AND TERRY'S GUIDE TO THE TREEHOUSE:

WHO'S WHO AND WHAT'S WHERE?

Explore the vast, surprising and silly world of the Treehouse with your expert tour guides, Andy and Terry. There are so many things to know. And so many things you didn't know you didn't know! This guide to the Treehouse is full of trivia, fun facts and behind-the-scenes details about all 169 levels, all the characters Andy and Terry have met, the places they've visited, and all the amazing gadgets and machines they've invented.

THE
13-STOREY
TREEHOUSE

BY THE INTERNATIONALLY BESTSELLING
ANDY GRIFFITHS
& TERRY DENTON

THE
26-STOREY
TREEHOUSE

BY THE INTERNATIONALLY BESTSELLING
ANDY GRIFFITHS

THE
39-STOREY
TREEHOUSE

BY THE INTERNATIONALLY BESTSELLING
ANDY GRIFFITHS

THE
52-STOREY
TREEHOUSE

BY THE INTERNATIONALLY BESTSELLING
ANDY GRIFFITHS
TERRY DENTON

THE
65-STOREY
TREEHOUSE

BY THE INTERNATIONALLY BESTSELLING
ANDY GRIFFITHS
& TERRY DENTON

THE
78-STOREY
TREEHOUSE

BY THE INTERNATIONALLY BESTSELLING
ANDY GRIFFITHS
& TERRY DENTON

THE
91-STOREY
TREEHOUSE

BY THE INTERNATIONALLY BESTSELLING
ANDY GRIFFITHS

THE
104-STOREY
TREEHOUSE

It's a
GIANT FOOT!

Get it
off me!

BY THE INTERNATIONALLY BESTSELLING
ANDY GRIFFITHS

THE
117-STOREY
TREEHOUSE

BY THE INTERNATIONALLY BESTSELLING
ANDY GRIFFITHS

THE
130-STOREY
TREEHOUSE

LASER EYES & ANNOYING FLIES!

ANDY GRIFFITHS
& TERRY DENTON

THE
143-STOREY
TREEHOUSE

CAMPING HOOTS AND SOGGY BOOTS!

OVER
10 MILLION
CHILDREN
LAUGHING
WORLDWIDE!

ANDY GRIFFITHS
& TERRY DENTON

THE
156-STOREY
TREEHOUSE

FESTIVE FROLICS AND SNEAKY SNOWMEN!

OVER
10 MILLION
CHILDREN
LAUGHING
WORLDWIDE!

ANDY GRIFFITHS
& TERRY DENTON